' Sentences to eat with
a spoon, and funny like
nothing else on earth '

Tilda Swinton

A WODEHOUSE
PG

Pick-Me-Up!

Goodbye
to All Cats

arrow books

1 3 5 7 9 10 8 6 4 2

Arrow Books
20 Vauxhall Bridge Road
London SW1V 2SA

Arrow Books is part of the Penguin Random House group of companies
whose addresses can be found at global.penguinrandomhouse.com

'Goodbye to All Cats' from *Young Men in Spats*, first published in the
United Kingdom by Herbert Jenkins Ltd in 1936
'Ukridge's Dog College' and 'Ukridge's Accident Syndicate' from *Ukridge*,
first published in the United Kingdom by Herbert Jenkins Ltd in 1924
Both collections published by Arrow Books in 2008
This collection first published in the United Kingdom by Arrow Books in 2017

www.penguin.co.uk

www.wodehouse.co.uk

A CIP catalogue record for this book is available from the British Library.

ISBN 9781787460133

Typeset in 12/14 pt Perpetua Std by Jouve (UK), Milton Keynes
Printed and bound in Great Britain by Clays Ltd, St Ives Plc

Penguin Random House is committed to a
sustainable future for our business, our readers
and our planet. This book is made from Forest
Stewardship Council® certified paper.

CONTENTS

GOODBYE TO ALL CATS

As the club kitten sauntered into the smoking-room of the Drones Club and greeted those present with a friendly miauw, Freddie Widgeon, who had been sitting in a corner with his head between his hands, rose stiffly.

'I had supposed,' he said, in a cold, level voice, 'that this was a quiet retreat for gentlemen. As I perceive that it is a blasted Zoo, I will withdraw.'

And he left the room in a marked manner.

There was a good deal of surprise, mixed with consternation.

'What's the trouble?' asked an Egg, concerned. Such exhibitions of the naked emotions are rare at the Drones. 'Have they had a row?'

A Crumpet, always well-informed, shook his head.

'Freddie has had no personal breach with this particular kitten,' he said. 'It is simply that since that week-end at Matcham Scratchings he can't stand the sight of a cat.'

'Matcham what?'

'Scratchings. The ancestral home of Dahlia Prenderby in Oxfordshire.'

'I met Dahlia Prenderby once,' said the Egg. 'I thought she seemed a nice girl.'

'Freddie thought so, too. He loved her madly.'

'And lost her, of course?'

'Absolutely.'

'Do you know,' said a thoughtful Bean, 'I'll bet that if all the girls Freddie Widgeon has loved and lost were placed end to end – not that I suppose one could do it – they would reach half-way down Piccadilly.'

'Further than that,' said the Egg. 'Some of them were pretty tall. What beats me is why he ever bothers to love them. They always turn him down in the end. He might just as well never begin. Better, in fact, because in the time saved he could be reading some good book.'

'I think the trouble with Freddie,' said the Crumpet, 'is that he always gets off to a flying start. He's a good-looking sort of chap who dances well and can wiggle his ears, and the girl is dazzled for the moment, and this encourages him. From what he tells me, he appears to have gone very big with this Prenderby girl at the outset. So much so, indeed, that when she invited him down to Matcham Scratchings he had already bought his copy of *What Every Young Bridegroom Ought To Know*.'

'Rummy, these old country-house names,' mused the Bean. 'Why Scratchings, I wonder?'

'Freddie wondered, too, till he got to the place. Then he tells me he felt it was absolutely the *mot juste*. This girl

2

Dahlia's family, you see, was one of those animal-loving families, and the house, he tells me, was just a frothing maelstrom of dumb chums. As far as the eye could reach, there were dogs scratching themselves and cats scratching the furniture. I believe, though he never met it socially, there was even a tame chimpanzee somewhere on the premises, no doubt scratching away as assiduously as the rest of them. You get these conditions here and there in the depths of the country, and this Matcham place was well away from the centre of things, being about six miles from the nearest station.

'It was at this station that Dahlia Prenderby met Freddie in her two-seater, and on the way to the house there occurred a conversation which I consider significant – showing, as it does, the cordial relations existing between the young couple at that point in the proceedings. I mean, it was only later that the bitter awakening and all that sort of thing popped up.'

'I do want you to be a success, Freddie,' said the girl, after talking a while of this and that. 'Some of the men I've asked down here have been such awful flops. The great thing is to make a good impression on Father.'

'I will,' said Freddie.

'He can be a little difficult at times.'

'Lead me to him,' said Freddie. 'That's all I ask. Lead me to him.'

'The trouble is, he doesn't much like young men.'

'He'll like me.'

'He will, will he?'

'Rather!'

'What makes you think that?'

'I'm a dashed fascinating chap.'

'Oh, you are?'

'Yes, I am.'

'You are, are you?'

'Rather!'

Upon which, she gave him a sort of push and he gave her a sort of push, and she giggled and he laughed like a paper bag bursting, and she gave him a kind of shove and he gave her a kind of shove, and she said, 'You *are* a silly ass!' and he said, 'What ho!' All of which shows you, I mean to say, the stage they had got to by this time. Nothing definitely settled, of course, but Love obviously beginning to burgeon in the girl's heart.

Well, naturally, Freddie gave a good deal of thought during the drive to this father of whom the girl had spoken so feelingly, and he resolved that he would not fail her. The way he would suck up to the old dad would be nobody's business. He proposed to exert upon him the full force of his magnetic personality, and looked forward to registering a very substantial hit.

Which being so, I need scarcely tell you, knowing Freddie as you do, that his first act on entering Sir Mortimer Prenderby's orbit was to make the scaliest kind of floater, hitting him on the back of the neck with a tortoiseshell cat not ten minutes after his arrival.

His train having been a bit late, there was no time on reaching the house for any stately receptions or any of that 'Welcome to Meadowsweet Hall' stuff. The girl simply shot him up to his room and told him to dress like a streak, because dinner was in a quarter of an hour, and then buzzed off to don the soup and fish herself. And Freddie was just going well when, looking round for his shirt, which he had left on the bed, he saw a large tortoiseshell cat standing on it, kneading it with its paws.

Well, you know how a fellow feels about his shirt-front. For an instant, Freddie stood spellbound. Then with a hoarse cry he bounded forward, scooped up the animal, and, carrying it out on to the balcony, flung it into the void. And an elderly gentleman, coming round the corner at this moment, received a direct hit on the back of his neck.

'Hell!' cried the elderly gentleman.

A head popped out of a window.

'Whatever is the matter, Mortimer?'

'It's raining cats.'

'Nonsense. It's a lovely evening,' said the head, and disappeared.

Freddie thought an apology would be in order.

'I say,' he said.

The old gentleman looked in every direction of the compass, and finally located Freddie on his balcony.

'I say,' said Freddie, 'I'm awfully sorry you got that nasty buffet. It was me.'

'It was not you. It was a cat.'

'I know. I threw the cat.'

'Why?'

'Well . . .'

'Dam' fool.'

'I'm sorry,' said Freddie.

'Go to blazes,' said the old gentleman.

Freddie backed into the room, and the incident closed.

Freddie is a pretty slippy dresser, as a rule, but this episode had shaken him, and he not only lost a collar-stud but made a mess of the first two ties. The result was that the gong went while he was still in his shirt-sleeves: and on emerging from his boudoir he was informed by a footman that the gang were already nuzzling their *bouillon* in the dining-room. He pushed straight on there, accordingly, and sank into a chair beside his hostess just in time to dead-heat with the final spoonful.

Awkward, of course, but he was feeling in pretty good form owing to the pleasantness of the thought that he was shoving his knees under the same board as the girl Dahlia: so, having nodded to his host, who was glaring at him from the head of the table, as much as to say that all would be explained in God's good time, he shot his cuffs and started to make sparkling conversation to Lady Prenderby.

'Charming place you have here, what?'

Lady Prenderby said that the local scenery was generally admired. She was one of those tall, rangy, Queen

Elizabeth sort of women, with tight lips and cold, blanc-mange-y eyes. Freddie didn't like her looks much, but he was feeling, as I say, fairly fizzy, so he carried on with a bright zip.

'Pretty good hunting country, I should think?'

'I believe there is a good deal of hunting near here, yes.'

'I thought as much,' said Freddie. 'Ah, that's the stuff, is it not? A cracking gallop across good country with a jolly fine kill at the end of it, what, what? Hark for'ard, yoicks, tally-ho, I mean to say, and all that sort of thing.'

Lady Prenderby shivered austerely.

'I fear I cannot share your enthusiasm,' she said. 'I have the strongest possible objection to hunting. I have always set my face against it, as against all similar brutalizing blood-sports.'

This was a nasty jar for poor old Freddie, who had been relying on the topic to carry him nicely through at least a couple of courses. It silenced him for the nonce. And as he paused to collect his faculties, his host, who had now been glowering for six and a half minutes practically without cessation, put a hand in front of his mouth and addressed the girl Dahlia across the table. Freddie thinks he was under the impression that he was speaking in a guarded whisper, but, as a matter of fact, the words boomed through the air as if he had been a costermonger calling attention to his Brussels sprouts.

'Dahlia!'

'Yes, Father?'

'Who's that ugly feller?'

'Hush!'

'What do you mean, hush? Who is he?'

'Mr Widgeon.'

'Mr Who?'

'Widgeon.'

'I wish you would articulate clearly and not mumble,' said Sir Mortimer fretfully. 'It sounds to me just like "Widgeon". Who asked him here?'

'I did.'

'Why?'

'He's a friend of mine.'

'Well, he looks a pretty frightful young slab of damnation to me. What I'd call a criminal face.'

'Hush!'

'Why do you keep saying "Hush"? Must be a lunatic, too. Throws cats at people.'

'Please, Father!'

'Don't say "Please, Father!" No sense in it. I tell you he does throw cats at people. He threw one at me. Half-witted, I'd call him – if that. Besides being the most offensive-looking young toad I've ever seen on the premises. How long's he staying?'

'Till Monday.'

'My God! And today's only Friday!' bellowed Sir Mortimer Prenderby.

It was an unpleasant situation for Freddie, of course,

and I'm bound to admit he didn't carry it off particularly well. What he ought to have done, obviously, was to have plunged into an easy flow of small-talk: but all he could think of was to ask Lady Prenderby if she was fond of shooting. Lady Prenderby having replied that, owing to being deficient in the savage instincts and wanton blood-lust that went to make up a callous and cold-hearted murderess, she was not, he relapsed into silence with his lower jaw hanging down.

All in all, he wasn't so dashed sorry when dinner came to an end.

As he and Sir Mortimer were the only men at the table, most of the seats having been filled by a covey of mildewed females whom he had classified under the general heading of Aunts, it seemed to Freddie that the moment had now arrived when they would be able to get together once more, under happier conditions than those of their last meeting, and start to learn to appreciate one another's true worth. He looked forward to a cosy *tête-à-tête* over the port, in the course of which he would smooth over that cat incident and generally do all that lay within his power to revise the unfavourable opinion of him which the other must have formed.

But apparently Sir Mortimer had his own idea of the duties and obligations of a host. Instead of clustering round Freddie with decanters, he simply gave him a long, lingering look of distaste and shot out of the french window into the garden. A moment later, his head reappeared and he uttered the words: 'You and your dam' cats!' Then the night swallowed him again.

Freddie was a good deal perplexed. All this was new stuff to him. He had been in and out of a number of country-houses in his time, but this was the first occasion on which he had ever been left flat at the conclusion of the evening meal, and he wasn't quite sure how to handle the situation. He was still wondering, when Sir Mortimer's head came into view again and its owner, after giving him another of those long, lingering looks, said: 'Cats, forsooth!' and disappeared once more.

Freddie was now definitely piqued. It was all very well, he felt, Dahlia Prenderby telling him to make himself solid with her father, but how can you make yourself solid with a fellow who doesn't stay put for a couple of consecutive seconds? If it was Sir Mortimer's intention to spend the remainder of the night flashing past like a merry-go-round, there seemed little hope of anything amounting to a genuine *rapprochement*. It was a relief to his feelings when there suddenly appeared from nowhere his old acquaintance the tortoiseshell cat. It seemed to offer to him a means of working off his spleen.

Taking from Lady Prenderby's plate, accordingly, the remains of a banana, he plugged the animal at a range of two yards. It yowled and withdrew. And a moment later, there was Sir Mortimer again.

'Did you kick that cat?' said Sir Mortimer.

Freddie had half a mind to ask this old disease if he

thought he was a man or a jack-in-the-box, but the breeding of the Widgeons restrained him.

'No,' he said, 'I did not kick that cat.'

'You must have done something to it to make it come charging out at forty miles an hour.'

'I merely offered the animal a piece of fruit.'

'Do it again and see what happens to you.'

'Lovely evening,' said Freddie, changing the subject.

'No, it's not, you silly ass,' said Sir Mortimer. Freddie rose. His nerve, I fancy, was a little shaken.

'I shall join the ladies,' he said, with dignity.

'God help them!' replied Sir Mortimer Prenderby in a voice instinct with the deepest feeling, and vanished once more.

Freddie's mood, as he made for the drawing-room, was thoughtful. I don't say he has much sense, but he's got enough to know when he is and when he isn't going with a bang. Tonight, he realized, he had been very far from going in such a manner. It was not, that is to say, as the Idol of Matcham Scratchings that he would enter the drawing-room, but rather as a young fellow who had made an unfortunate first impression and would have to do a lot of heavy ingratiating before he could regard himself as really popular in the home.

He must bustle about, he felt, and make up leeway. And, knowing that what counts with these old-style females who have lived in the country all their lives is the exhibition of those little politenesses and attentions which were all the go in Queen Victoria's time, his first action, on entering, was to make a dive for one of the aunts who seemed to be trying to find a place to put her coffee-cup.

'Permit me,' said Freddie, suave to the eyebrows.

And bounding forward with the feeling that this was the stuff to give them, he barged right into a cat.

'Oh, sorry,' he said, backing and bringing down his heel on another cat.

'I say, most frightfully sorry,' he said.

And, tottering to a chair, he sank heavily on to a third cat.

Well, he was up and about again in a jiffy, of course, but it was too late. There was the usual not-at-all-ing and don't-mention-it-ing, but he could read between the lines. Lady Prenderby's eyes had rested on his for only a brief instant, but it had been enough. His standing with her, he perceived, was now approximately what King Herod's would have been at an Israelite Mothers Social Saturday Afternoon.

The girl Dahlia during these exchanges had been sitting on a sofa at the end of the room, turning the pages of a weekly paper, and the sight of her drew Freddie like a magnet. Her womanly sympathy was just what he felt he could do with at this juncture. Treading with infinite caution, he crossed to where she sat: and, having scanned the terrain narrowly for cats, sank down on the sofa at her side. And conceive his agony of spirit when he discovered that womanly sympathy had been turned off at the main. The girl was like a chunk of ice-cream with spikes all over it.

'Please do not trouble to explain,' she said coldly, in answer to his opening words. 'I quite understand that there are people who have this odd dislike of animals.'

'But, dash it . . .' cried Freddie, waving his arm in a frenzied sort of way. 'Oh, I say, sorry,' he added, as his fist sloshed another of the menagerie in the short ribs.

Dahlia caught the animal as it flew through the air.

'I think perhaps you had better take Augustus, Mother,' she said. 'He seems to be annoying Mr Widgeon.'

'Quite,' said Lady Prenderby. 'He will be safer with me.'

'But, dash it . . .' bleated Freddie.

Dahlia Prenderby drew in her breath sharply.

'How true it is,' she said, 'that one never really knows a man till after one has seen him in one's own home.'

'What do you mean by that?'

'Oh, nothing,' said Dahlia Prenderby.

She rose and moved to the piano, where she proceeded to sing old Breton folk-songs in a distant manner, leaving Freddie to make out as best he could with a family album containing faded photographs with 'Aunt Emily bathing at Llandudno, 1893', and 'This is Cousin George at the fancy-dress ball' written under them.

And so the long, quiet, peaceful home evening wore on, till eventually Lady Prenderby mercifully blew the whistle and he was at liberty to sneak off to his bedroom.

*

You might have supposed that Freddie's thoughts, as he toddled upstairs with his candle, would have dwelt exclusively on the girl Dahlia. This, however, was not so. He did give her obvious shirtiness a certain measure of attention, of course, but what really filled his mind was the soothing reflection that at long last his path and that of the animal kingdom of Matcham Scratchings had now divided. He, so to speak, was taking the high road while they, as it were, would take the low road. For whatever might be the conditions prevailing in the dining-room, the drawing-room, and the rest of the house, his bedroom, he felt, must surely be a haven totally free from cats of all descriptions.

Remembering, however, that unfortunate episode before dinner, he went down on all fours and subjected the various nooks and crannies to a close examination. His eye could detect no cats. Relieved, he rose to his feet with a gay song on his lips: and he hadn't got much beyond the first couple of bars when a voice behind him suddenly started taking the bass: and, turning, he perceived on the bed a fine Alsatian dog.

Freddie looked at the dog. The dog looked at Freddie. The situation was one fraught with embarrassment. A glance at the animal was enough to convince him that it had got an entirely wrong angle on the position of affairs and was regarding him purely in the light of an intrusive stranger who had muscled in on its private sleeping quarters. Its manner was plainly resentful. It fixed Freddie with a cold, yellow eye and curled its upper lip slightly, the better to display a long, white tooth. It also twitched its nose and gave a *sotto-voce* imitation of distant thunder.

Freddie did not know quite what avenue to explore. It was impossible to climb between the sheets with a thing like that on the counterpane. To spend the night in a chair, on the other hand, would have been foreign to his policy. He did what I consider the most statesmanlike thing by sidling out on to the balcony and squinting along the wall of the house to see if there wasn't a lighted window hard by, behind which might lurk somebody who would rally round with aid and comfort.

There was a lighted window only a short distance away, so he shoved his head out as far as it would stretch and said:

'I say!'

There being no response, he repeated:

'I say!'

And, finally, to drive his point home, he added:

'I say! I say! I say!'

This time he got results. The head of Lady Prenderby suddenly protruded from the window.

'Who,' she enquired, 'is making that abominable noise?'

It was not precisely the attitude Freddie had hoped for, but he could take the rough with the smooth.

'It's me. Widgeon, Frederick.'

'Must you sing on your balcony, Mr Widgeon?'

'I wasn't singing. I was saying "I say".'

'What were you saying?'

'"I say".'

'You say what?'

'I say I was saying "I say". Kind of a heart-cry, if you know what I mean. The fact is, there's a dog in my room.'

'What sort of dog?'

'A whacking great Alsatian.'

'Ah, that would be Wilhelm. Good night, Mr Widgeon.'

The window closed. Freddie let out a heart-stricken yip.

'But I say!'

The window reopened. 'Really, Mr Widgeon!'

'But what am I to do?'

'Do?'

'About this whacking great Alsatian!'

Lady Prenderby seemed to consider.

'No sweet biscuits,' she said. 'And when the maid brings you your tea in the morning please do not give him sugar. Simply a little milk in the saucer. He is on a diet. Good night, Mr Widgeon.'

Freddie was now pretty well nonplussed. No matter what his hostess might say about this beastly dog being on a diet, he was convinced from its manner that its medical adviser had not forbidden it Widgeons, and once more he bent his brain to the task of ascertaining what to do next.

There were several possible methods of procedure.

His balcony being not so very far from the ground, he could, if he pleased, jump down and pass a health-giving night in the nasturtium bed. Or he might curl up on the floor. Or he might get out of the room and doss downstairs somewhere.

This last scheme seemed about the best. The only obstacle in the way of its fulfilment was the fact that, when he started for the door, his room-mate would probably think he was a burglar about to loot silver of lonely country-house and pin him. Still, it had to be risked, and a moment later he might have been observed tiptoeing across the carpet, with all the caution of a slack-wire artist who isn't any too sure he remembers the correct steps.

Well, it was a near thing. At the instant when he started, the dog seemed occupied with something that looked like a cushion on the bed. It was licking this object in a thoughtful way, and paid no attention to Freddie till he was half-way across No Man's Land. Then it suddenly did a sort of sitting high-jump in his direction, and two seconds later Freddie, with a draughty feeling about the seat of his trouserings, was on top of a wardrobe, with the dog underneath looking up. He tells me that if he ever moved quicker in his life it was only on the occasion when, a lad of fourteen, he was discovered by his uncle, Lord Blicester, smoking one of the latter's cigars in the library: and he rather thinks he must have clipped at least a fifth of a second off the record then set up.

It looked to him now as if his sleeping arrangements

for the night had been settled for him. And the thought of having to roost on top of a wardrobe at the whim of a dog was pretty dashed offensive to his proud spirit, as you may well imagine. However, as you cannot reason with Alsatians, it seemed the only thing to be done: and he was trying to make himself as comfortable as a sharp piece of wood sticking into the fleshy part of his leg would permit, when there was a snuffling noise in the passage and through the door came an object which in the dim light he was at first not able to identify. It looked something like a pen-wiper and something like a piece of a hearth-rug. A second and keener inspection revealed it as a Pekingese puppy.

The uncertainty which Freddie had felt as to the newcomer's status was shared, it appeared, by the Alsatian: for after raising its eyebrows in a puzzled manner it rose and advanced enquiringly. In a tentative way it put out a paw and rolled the intruder over. Then, advancing again, it lowered its nose and sniffed.

It was a course of action against which its best friends would have advised it. These Pekes are tough eggs, especially when, as in this case, female. They look the world in the eye, and are swift to resent familiarity. There was a sort of explosion, and the next moment the Alsatian was shooting out of the room with its tail between its legs, hotly pursued. Freddie could hear the noise of battle rolling away along the passage, and it was music to his ears. Something on these lines was precisely what that Alsatian had been asking for, and now it had got it.

Presently, the Peke returned, dashing the beads of perspiration from its forehead, and came and sat down under the wardrobe, wagging a stumpy tail. And Freddie, feeling that the All Clear had been blown and that he was now at liberty to descend, did so.

His first move was to shut the door, his second to fraternize with his preserver. Freddie is a chap who believes in giving credit where credit is due, and it seemed to him that this Peke had shown itself an ornament of its species. He spared no effort, accordingly, to entertain it. He lay down on the floor and let it lick his face two hundred and thirty-three times. He tickled it under the left ear, the right ear, and at the base of the tail, in the order named. He also scratched its stomach.

All these attentions the animal received with cordiality and marked gratification: and as it seemed still in pleasure-seeking mood and had come to look upon him as the official Master of the Revels, Freddie, feeling that he could not disappoint it but must play the host no matter what the cost to himself, took off his tie and handed it over. He would not have done it for everybody, he says, but where this life-saving Peke was concerned the sky was the limit.

Well, the tie went like a breeze. It was a success from the start. The Peke chewed it and chased it and got entangled in it and dragged it about the room, and was just starting to shake it from side to side when an unfortunate thing happened. Misjudging its distance, it banged its head a nasty wallop against the leg of the bed.

There is nothing of the Red Indian at the stake about a puppy in circumstances like this. A moment later, Freddie's blood was chilled by a series of fearful shrieks that seemed to ring through the night like the dying cries of the party of the second part to a first-class murder. It amazed him that a mere Peke, and a juvenile Peke at that, should have been capable of producing such an uproar. He says that a Baronet, stabbed in the back with a paper-knife in his library, could not have made half such a row.

Eventually, the agony seemed to abate. Quite suddenly, as if nothing had happened, the Peke stopped yelling and with an amused smile started to play with the tie again. And at the same moment there was a sound of whispering outside, and then a knock at the door.

'Hullo?' said Freddie.

'It is I, sir. Biggleswade.'

'Who's Biggleswade?'

'The butler, sir.'

'What do you want?'

'Her ladyship wishes me to remove the dog which you are torturing.'

There was more whispering.

'Her ladyship also desires me to say that she will be reporting the affair in the morning to the Society for the Prevention of Cruelty to Animals.'

There was another spot of whispering.

'Her ladyship further instructs me to add that, should you prove recalcitrant, I am to strike you over the head with the poker.'

Well, you can't say this was pleasant for poor old Freddie, and he didn't think so himself. He opened the door, to perceive, without, a group consisting of Lady Prenderby, her daughter Dahlia, a few assorted aunts, and the butler, with poker. And he says he met Dahlia's eyes and they went through him like a knife.

'Let me explain . . .' he began.

'Spare us the details,' said Lady Prenderby with a shiver. She scooped up the Peke and felt it for broken bones.

'But listen . . .'

'Good night, Mr Widgeon.'

The aunts said good night, too, and so did the butler. The girl Dahlia preserved a revolted silence.

'But, honestly, it was nothing, really. It banged its head against the bed . . .'

'What did he say?' asked one of the aunts, who was a little hard of hearing.

'He says he banged the poor creature's head against the bed,' said Lady Prenderby.

'Dreadful!' said the aunt.

'Hideous!' said a second aunt.

A third aunt opened up another line of thought. She said that with men like Freddie in the house, was anyone safe? She mooted the possibility of them all being murdered in their beds. And though Freddie offered to give her a written guarantee that he hadn't the slightest intention of going anywhere near her bed, the idea seemed to make a deep impression.

'Biggleswade,' said Lady Prenderby.

'M'lady?'

'You will remain in this passage for the remainder of the night with your poker.'

'Very good, m'lady.'

'Should this man attempt to leave his room, you will strike him smartly over the head.'

'Just so, m'lady.'

'But, listen . . .' said Freddie.

'Good night, Mr Widgeon.'

The mob scene broke up. Soon the passage was empty save for Biggleswade the butler, who had begun to pace up and down, halting every now and then to flick the air with his poker as if testing the lissomness of his wrist-muscles and satisfying himself that they were in a condition to ensure the right amount of follow-through.

The spectacle he presented was so unpleasant that Freddie withdrew into his room and shut the door. His bosom, as you may imagine, was surging with distressing emotions. That look which Dahlia Prenderby had given him had churned him up to no little extent. He realized that he had a lot of tense thinking to do, and to assist thought he sat down on the bed.

Or, rather, to be accurate, on the dead cat which was lying on the bed. It was this cat which the Alsatian had been licking just before the final breach in his relations with Freddie – the object, if you remember, which the latter had supposed to be a cushion.

He leaped up as if the corpse, instead of being cold,

had been piping hot. He stared down, hoping against hope that the animal was merely in some sort of coma. But a glance told him that it had made the great change. He had never seen a deader cat. After life's fitful fever it slept well.

You wouldn't be far out in saying that poor old Freddie was now appalled. Already his reputation in this house was at zero, his name mud. On all sides he was looked upon as Widgeon the Amateur Vivisectionist. This final disaster could not but put the tin hat on it. Before, he had had a faint hope that in the morning, when calmer moods would prevail, he might be able to explain that matter of the Peke. But who was going to listen to him if he were discovered with a dead cat on his person?

And then the thought came to him that it might be possible not to be discovered with it on his person. He had only to nip downstairs and deposit the remains in the drawing-room or somewhere and suspicion might not fall upon him. After all, in a super-catted house like this, cats must always be dying like flies all over the place. A housemaid would find the animal in the morning and report to G.H.Q. that the cat strength of the establishment had been reduced by one, and there would be a bit of tut-tutting and perhaps a silent tear or two, and then the thing would be forgotten.

The thought gave him new life. All briskness and efficiency, he picked up the body by the tail and was just about to dash out of the room when, with a silent groan, he remembered Biggleswade.

23

He peeped out. It might be that the butler, once the eye of authority had been removed, had departed to get the remainder of his beauty-sleep. But no. Service and Fidelity were evidently the watchwords at Matcham Scratchings. There the fellow was, still practising half-arm shots with the poker. Freddie closed the door.

And, as he did so, he suddenly thought of the window. There lay the solution. Here he had been, fooling about with doors and thinking in terms of drawing-rooms, and all the while there was the balcony staring him in the face. All he had to do was to shoot the body out into the silent night, and let gardeners, not house-maids, discover it.

He hurried out. It was a moment for swift action. He raised his burden. He swung it to and fro, working up steam. Then he let it go, and from the dark garden there came suddenly the cry of a strong man in his anger.

'Who threw that cat?'

It was the voice of his host, Sir Mortimer Prenderby.

'Show me the man who threw that cat!' he thundered.

Windows flew up. Heads came out. Freddie sank to the floor of the balcony and rolled against the wall.

'Whatever is the matter, Mortimer?'

'Let me get at the man who hit me in the eye with a cat.'

'A cat?' Lady Prenderby's voice sounded perplexed. 'Are you sure?'

'Sure? What do you mean sure? Of course I'm sure.

I was just dropping off to sleep in my hammock, when suddenly a great beastly cat came whizzing through the air and caught me properly in the eyeball. It's a nice thing. A man can't sleep in hammocks in his own garden without people pelting him with cats. I insist on the blood of the man who threw that cat.'

'Where did it come from?'

'Must have come from that balcony there.'

'Mr Widgeon's balcony,' said Lady Prenderby in an acid voice. 'As I might have guessed.'

Sir Mortimer uttered a cry.

'So might I have guessed! Widgeon, of course! That ugly feller. He's been throwing cats all the evening. I've got a nasty sore place on the back of my neck where he hit me with one before dinner. Somebody come and open the front door. I want my heavy cane, the one with the carved ivory handle. Or a horsewhip will do.'

'Wait, Mortimer,' said Lady Prenderby. 'Do nothing rash. The man is evidently a very dangerous lunatic. I will send Biggleswade to overpower him. He has the kitchen poker.'

Little (said the Crumpet) remains to be told. At two-fifteen that morning a sombre figure in dress clothes without a tie limped into the little railway station of Lower-Smattering-on-the-Wissel, some six miles from Matcham Scratchings. At three-forty-seven it departed Londonwards on the up milk-train. It was Frederick Widgeon. He had a broken heart and blisters on both heels. And in that broken heart was that loathing for all cats of which you recently saw so signal a manifestation. I am revealing no secrets when I tell you that Freddie Widgeon is permanently through with cats. From now on, they cross his path at their peril.

'Laddie,' said Stanley Featherstonehaugh Ukridge, that much-enduring man, helping himself to my tobacco and slipping the pouch absently into his pocket, 'listen to me, you son of Belial.'

'What?' I said, retrieving the pouch.

'Do you want to make an enormous fortune?'

'I do.'

'Then write my biography. Bung it down on paper, and we'll split the proceeds. I've been making a pretty close study of your stuff lately, old horse, and it's all wrong. The trouble with you is that you don't plumb the well-springs of human nature and all that. You just think up some rotten yarn about some-dam'-thing-or-other and shove it down. Now, if you tackled my life, you'd have something worth writing about. Pots of money in it, my boy — English serial rights and American serial rights and book rights, and dramatic rights and movie rights — well, you can take it from me that, at a conservative estimate, we should clean up at least fifty thousand pounds apiece.'

'As much as that?'

'Fully that. And listen, laddie, I'll tell you what. You're a good chap and we've been pals for years, so I'll let you have my share of the English serial rights for a hundred pounds down.'

'What makes you think I've got a hundred pounds?'

'Well, then, I'll make it my share of the English *and* American serial rights for fifty.'

'Your collar's come off its stud.'

'How about my complete share of the whole dashed outfit for twenty-five?'

'Not for me, thanks.'

'Then I'll tell you what, old horse,' said Ukridge, inspired. 'Just lend me half a crown to be going on with.'

If the leading incidents of S. F. Ukridge's disreputable career are to be given to the public – and not, as some might suggest, decently hushed up – I suppose I am the man to write them. Ukridge and I have been intimate since the days of school. Together we sported on the green, and when he was expelled no one missed him more than I. An unfortunate business, this expulsion. Ukridge's generous spirit, ever ill-attuned to school rules, caused him eventually to break the solemnest of them all by sneaking out at night to try his skill at the coconut-shies of the local village fair; and his foresight in putting on scarlet whiskers and a false nose for the expedition was completely neutralized by the fact that he absent-mindedly wore his school cap throughout the entire proceedings. He left the next morning, regretted by all.

After this there was a hiatus of some years in our friendship. I was at Cambridge, absorbing culture, and Ukridge, as far as I could gather from his rare letters and the reports of mutual acquaintances, flitting about the world like a snipe. Somebody met him in New York, just off a cattle-ship. Somebody else saw him in Buenos Ayres. Somebody, again, spoke sadly of having been pounced on by him at Monte Carlo and touched for a fiver. It was not until I settled down in London that he came back into my life. We met in Piccadilly one day, and resumed our relations where they had been broken off. Old associations are strong, and the fact that he was about my build and so could wear my socks and shirts drew us very close together.

Then he disappeared again, and it was a month or more before I got news of him.

It was George Tupper who brought the news. George was head of the school in my last year, and he has fulfilled exactly the impeccable promise of those early days. He is in the Foreign Office, doing well and much respected. He has an earnest, pulpy heart and takes other people's troubles very seriously. Often he had mourned to me like a father over Ukridge's erratic progress through life, and now, as he spoke, he seemed to be filled with a solemn joy, as over a reformed prodigal.

'Have you heard about Ukridge?' said George Tupper. 'He has settled down at last. Gone to live with an aunt of his who owns one of those big houses on

Wimbledon Common. A very rich woman. I am delighted. It will be the making of the old chap.'

I suppose he was right in a way, but to me this tame subsidence into companionship with a rich aunt in Wimbledon seemed somehow an indecent, almost a tragic, end to a colourful career like that of S. F. Ukridge. And when I met the man a week later my heart grew heavier still.

It was in Oxford Street at the hour when women come up from the suburbs to shop; and he was standing among the dogs and commissionaires outside Selfridge's. His arms were full of parcels, his face was set in a mask of wan discomfort, and he was so beautifully dressed that for an instant I did not recognize him. Everything which the Correct Man wears was assembled on his person, from the silk hat to the patent-leather boots; and, as he confided to me in the first minute, he was suffering the tortures of the damned. The boots pinched him, the hat hurt his forehead, and the collar was worse than the hat and boots combined.

'She makes me wear them,' he said, moodily, jerking his head towards the interior of the store and uttering a sharp howl as the movement caused the collar to gouge his neck.

'Still,' I said, trying to turn his mind to happier things, 'you must be having a great time. George Tupper tells me that your aunt is rich. I suppose you're living off the fat of the land.'

'The browsing and sluicing are good,' admitted

Ukridge. 'But it's a wearing life, laddie. A wearing life, old horse.'

'Why don't you come and see me sometimes?'

'I'm not allowed out at night.'

'Well, shall I come and see you?'

A look of poignant alarm shot out from under the silk hat.

'Don't dream of it, laddie,' said Ukridge, earnestly. 'Don't dream of it. You're a good chap — my best pal and all that sort of thing — but the fact is, my standing in the home's none too solid even now, and one sight of you would knock my prestige into hash. Aunt Julia would think you worldly.'

'I'm not worldly.'

'Well, you look worldly. You wear a squash hat and a soft collar. If you don't mind my suggesting it, old horse, I think, if I were you, I'd pop off now before she comes out. Good-bye, laddie.'

'Ichabod!' I murmured sadly to myself as I passed on down Oxford Street. 'Ichabod!'

I should have had more faith. I should have known my Ukridge better. I should have realized that a London suburb could no more imprison that great man permanently than Elba did Napoleon.

One afternoon, as I let myself into the house in Ebury Street of which I rented at that time the bedroom and sitting-room on the first floor, I came upon Bowles, my landlord, standing in listening attitude at the foot of the stairs.

'Good afternoon, sir,' said Bowles. 'A gentleman is waiting to see you. I fancy I heard him calling me a moment ago.'

'Who is he?'

'A Mr Ukridge, sir. He—'

A vast voice boomed out from above.

'Bowles, old horse!'

Bowles, like all other proprietors of furnished apartments in the south-western district of London, was an ex-butler, and about him, as about all ex-butlers, there clung like a garment an aura of dignified superiority which had never failed to crush my spirit. He was a man of portly aspect, with a bald head and prominent eyes of a lightish green – eyes that seemed to weigh me dispassionately and find me wanting. 'H'm!' they seemed to say. 'Young – very young. And not at all what I have been accustomed to in the best places.' To hear this dignitary addressed – and in a shout at that – as 'old horse' affected me with much the same sense of imminent chaos as would afflict a devout young curate if he saw his bishop slapped on the back. The shock, therefore, when he responded not merely mildly but with what almost amounted to camaraderie was numbing.

'Sir?' cooed Bowles.

'Bring me six bones and a corkscrew.'

'Very good, sir.'

Bowles retired, and I bounded upstairs and flung open the door of my sitting-room.

'Great Scott!' I said, blankly.

The place was a sea of Pekingese dogs. Later investigation reduced their numbers to six, but in that first moment there seemed to be hundreds. Goggling eyes met mine wherever I looked. The room was a forest of waving tails. With his back against the mantelpiece, smoking placidly, stood Ukridge.

'Hallo, laddie!' he said, with a genial wave of the hand, as if to make me free of the place. 'You're just in time. I've got to dash off and catch a train in a quarter of an hour. Stop it, you mutts!' he bellowed, and the six Pekingese, who had been barking steadily since my arrival, stopped in mid-yap, and were still. Ukridge's personality seemed to exercise a magnetism over the animal kingdom, from ex-butlers to Pekes, which bordered on the uncanny. 'I'm off to Sheep's Cray, in Kent. Taken a cottage there.'

'Are you going to live there?'

'Yes.'

'But what about your aunt?'

'Oh, I've left her. Life is stern and life is earnest, and if I mean to make a fortune I've got to bustle about and not stay cooped up in a place like Wimbledon.'

'Something in that.'

'Besides which, she told me the very sight of me made her sick and she never wanted to see me again.'

I might have guessed, directly I saw him, that some upheaval had taken place. The sumptuous raiment which had made him such a treat to the eye at our last meeting was gone, and he was back in his pre-Wimbledon costume, which was, as the advertisements say, distinctly individual. Over grey flannel trousers, a golf coat, and a brown sweater he wore like a royal robe a bright yellow mackintosh. His collar had broken free from its stud and showed a couple of inches of bare neck. His hair was disordered, and his masterful nose was topped by a pair of steel-rimmed pince-nez cunningly attached to his flapping ears with ginger-beer wire. His whole appearance spelled revolt.

Bowles manifested himself with a plateful of bones.

'That's right. Chuck 'em down on the floor.'

'Very good, sir.'

'I like that fellow,' said Ukridge, as the door closed. 'We had a dashed interesting talk before you came in. Did you know he had a cousin on the music-halls?'

'He hasn't confided in me much.'

'He's promised me an introduction to him later on. May be useful to be in touch with a man who knows the ropes. You see, laddie, I've hit on the most amazing scheme.' He swept his arm round dramatically, overturning a plaster cast of the Infant Samuel at Prayer. 'All right, all right, you can mend it with glue or something, and anyway, you're probably better without it. Yessir, I've hit on a great scheme. The idea of a thousand years.'

'What's that?'

'I'm going to train dogs.'

'Train dogs?'

'For the music-hall stage. Dog acts, you know.

Performing dogs. Pots of money in it. I start in a modest way with these six. When I've taught 'em a few tricks, I sell them to a fellow in the profession for a large sum and buy twelve more. I train those, sell 'em for a large sum, and with the money buy twenty-four more. I train those—'

'Here, wait a minute.' My head was beginning to swim. I had a vision of England paved with Pekingese dogs, all doing tricks. 'How do you know you'll be able to sell them?'

'Of course I shall. The demand's enormous. Supply can't cope with it. At a conservative estimate I should think I ought to scoop in four or five thousand pounds the first year. That, of course, is before the business really starts to expand.'

'I see.'

'When I get going properly, with a dozen assistants under me and an organized establishment, I shall begin to touch the big money. What I'm aiming at is a sort of Dog's College out in the country somewhere. Big place with a lot of ground. Regular classes and a set curriculum. Large staff, each member of it with so many dogs under his care, me looking on and superintending. Why, once the thing starts moving it'll run itself, and all I shall have to do will be to sit back and endorse the cheques. It isn't as if I would have to confine my operations to England. The demand for performing dogs is universal throughout the civilized world. America wants performing dogs. Australia wants performing dogs. Africa could do with a few, I've no doubt. My aim, laddie, is gradually to get a monopoly of the trade. I want everybody who needs a performing dog of any description to come automatically to me. And I'll tell you what, laddie. If you like to put up a bit of capital, I'll let you in on the ground floor.'

'No, thanks.'

'All right. Have it your own way. Only don't forget that there was a fellow who put nine hundred dollars into the Ford Car business when it was starting and he collected a cool forty million. I say, is that clock right? Great Scott! I'll be missing my train. Help me mobilize these dashed animals.'

Five minutes later, accompanied by the six Pekingese and bearing about him a pound of my tobacco, three pairs of my socks, and the remains of a bottle of whisky, Ukridge departed in a taxi-cab for Charing Cross Station to begin his life-work.

Perhaps six weeks passed, six quiet Ukridgeless weeks, and then one morning I received an agitated telegram. Indeed, it was not so much a telegram as a cry of anguish. In every word of it there breathed the tortured spirit of a great man who has battled in vain against overwhelming odds. It was the sort of telegram which Job might have sent off after a lengthy session with Bildad the Shuhite:

Come here immediately, laddie. Life and death matter, old horse. Desperate situation. Don't fail me.

It stirred me like a bugle: I caught the next train.

The White Cottage, Sheep's Cray — destined, presumably, to become in future years an historic spot and a Mecca for dog-loving pilgrims — was a small and battered building standing near the main road to London at some distance from the village. I found it without difficulty, for Ukridge seemed to have achieved a certain celebrity in the neighbourhood; but to effect an entry was a harder task. I rapped for a full minute without result, then shouted; and I was about to conclude that Ukridge was not at home when the door suddenly opened. As I was just giving a final bang at the moment, I entered the house in a manner reminiscent of one of the Ballet Russe practising a new and difficult step.

'Sorry, old horse,' said Ukridge. 'Wouldn't have kept you waiting if I'd known who it was. Thought you were Gooch, the grocer — goods supplied to the value of six pounds three and a penny.'

'I see.'

'He keeps hounding me for his beastly money,' said Ukridge, bitterly, as he led the way into the sitting-room. 'It's a little hard. Upon my Sam it's a little hard. I come down here to inaugurate a vast business and do the natives a bit of good by establishing a growing industry in their midst, and the first thing you know they turn round and bite the hand that was going to feed them. I've been hampered and rattled by these blood-suckers ever since I got here. A little trust, a little sympathy, a little of the good old give-and-take

37

spirit – that was all I asked. And what happened? They wanted a bit on account! Kept bothering me for a bit on account, I'll trouble you, just when I needed all my thoughts and all my energy and every ounce of concentration at my command for my extraordinarily difficult and delicate work. *I* couldn't give them a bit on account. Later on, if they had only exercised reasonable patience, I would no doubt have been in a position to settle their infernal bills fifty times over. But the time was not ripe. I reasoned with the men. I said, "Here am I, a busy man, trying hard to educate six Pekingese dogs for the music-hall stage, and you come distracting my attention and impairing my efficiency by babbling about a bit on account. It isn't the pull-together spirit," I said. "It isn't the spirit that wins to wealth. These narrow petty-cash ideas can never make for success." But no, they couldn't see it. They started calling here at all hours and waylaying me in the public highways till life became an absolute curse. And now what do you think has happened?'

'What?'

'The dogs.'

'Got distemper?'

'No. Worse. My landlord's pinched them as security for his infernal rent! Sneaked the stock. Tied up the assets. Crippled the business at the very outset. Have you ever in your life heard of anything so dastardly? I know I agreed to pay the damned rent weekly and I'm about six weeks behind, but, my gosh! surely a man with a huge enterprise on his hands isn't supposed to have to worry about these trifles when he's occupied with the most delicate – Well, I put all that to old Nickerson, but a fat lot of good it did. So then I wired to you.'

'Ah!' I said, and there was a brief and pregnant pause.

'I thought,' said Ukridge, meditatively, 'that you might be able to suggest somebody I could touch.'

He spoke in a detached and almost casual way, but his eye was gleaming at me significantly, and I avoided it with a sense of guilt. My finances at the moment were in their customary unsettled condition – rather more so, in fact, than usual, owing to unsatisfactory speculations at Kempton Park on the previous Saturday; and it seemed to me that, if ever there was a time for passing the buck, this was it. I mused tensely. It was an occasion for quick thinking.

'George Tupper!' I cried, on the crest of a brain-wave.

'George Tupper?' echoed Ukridge, radiantly, his gloom melting like a fog before the sun. 'The very man, by Gad! It's a most amazing thing, but I never thought of him. George Tupper, of course! Big-hearted George, the old school-chum. He'll do it like a shot and won't miss the money. These Foreign Office blokes have always got a spare tenner or two tucked away in the old sock. They pinch it out of the public funds. Rush back to town, laddie, with all speed, get hold of Tuppy, lush him up, and bite his ear for twenty quid. Now is the time for all good men to come to the aid of the party.'

I had been convinced that George Tupper would not fail us, nor did he. He parted without a murmur – even with enthusiasm. The consignment was one that might have been made to order for him. As a boy, George used to write sentimental poetry for the school magazine, and now he is the sort of man who is always starting subscription lists and getting up memorials and presentations. He listened to my story with the serious official air which these Foreign Office fellows put on when they are deciding whether to declare war on Switzerland or send a firm note to San Marino, and was reaching for his cheque-book before I had been speaking two minutes. Ukridge's sad case seemed to move him deeply.

'Too bad,' said George. 'So he is training dogs, is he? Well, it seems very unfair that, if he has at last settled down to real work, he should be hampered by financial difficulties at the outset. We ought to do something practical for him. After all, a loan of twenty pounds cannot relieve the situation permanently.'

'I think you're a bit optimistic if you're looking on it as a loan.'

'What Ukridge needs is capital.'

'He thinks that, too. So does Gooch, the grocer.'

'Capital,' repeated George Tupper, firmly, as if he were reasoning with the plenipotentiary of some Great Power. 'Every venture requires capital at first.' He frowned thoughtfully. 'Where can we obtain capital for Ukridge?'

'Rob a bank.'

George Tupper's face cleared.

'I have it!' he said. 'I will go straight over to Wimbledon tonight and approach his aunt.'

'Aren't you forgetting that Ukridge is about as popular with her as a cold welsh rabbit?'

'There may be a temporary estrangement, but if I tell her the facts and impress upon her that Ukridge is really making a genuine effort to earn a living—'

'Well, try it if you like. But she will probably set the parrot on to you.'

'It will have to be done diplomatically, of course. It might be as well if you did not tell Ukridge what I propose to do. I do not wish to arouse hopes which may not be fulfilled.'

A blaze of yellow on the platform of Sheep's Cray Station next morning informed me that Ukridge had come to meet my train. The sun poured down from a cloudless sky, but it took more than sunshine to make Stanley Featherstonehaugh Ukridge discard his mackintosh. He looked like an animated blob of mustard.

When the train rolled in, he was standing in solitary grandeur trying to light his pipe, but as I got out I perceived that he had been joined by a sad-looking man, who, from the rapid and earnest manner in which he talked and the vehemence of his gesticulations, appeared to be ventilating some theme on which he felt deeply. Ukridge was looking warm and harassed, and, as I approached, I could hear his voice booming in reply.

'My dear sir, my dear old horse, do be reasonable, do try to cultivate the big, broad flexible outlook —'

He saw me and broke away — not unwillingly; and, gripping my arm, drew me off along the platform. The sad-looking man followed irresolutely.

'Have you got the stuff, laddie?' inquired Ukridge, in a tense whisper. 'Have you got it?'

'Yes, here it is.'

'Put it back, put it back!' moaned Ukridge in agony, as I felt in my pocket. 'Do you know who that was I was talking to? Gooch, the grocer!'

'Goods supplied to the value of six pounds three and a penny?'

'Absolutely!'

'Well, now's your chance. Fling him a purse of gold. That'll make him look silly.'

'My dear old horse, I can't afford to go about the place squandering my cash simply in order to make grocers look silly. That money is earmarked for Nickerson, my landlord.'

'Oh! I say, I think the six-pounds-three-and-a-penny bird is following us.'

'Then for goodness' sake, laddie, let's get a move on! If that man knew we had twenty quid on us, our lives wouldn't be safe. He'd make one spring.'

He hurried me out of the station and led the way up a shady lane that wound off through the fields, slinking furtively 'like one that on a lonesome road doth walk in fear and dread, and having once looked back walks

42

on and turns no more his head, because he knows a frightful fiend doth close behind him tread'. As a matter of fact, the frightful fiend had given up the pursuit after the first few steps, and a moment later I drew this fact to Ukridge's attention, for it was not the sort of day on which to break walking records unnecessarily.

He halted, relieved, and mopped his spacious brow with a handkerchief which I recognized as having once been my property.

'Thank goodness we've shaken him off,' he said. 'Not a bad chap in his way, I believe – a good husband and father, I'm told, and sings in the church choir. But no vision. That's what he lacks, old horse – vision. He can't understand that all vast industrial enterprises have been built up on a system of liberal and cheerful credit. Won't realize that credit is the life-blood of commerce. Without credit commerce has no elasticity. And if commerce has no elasticity what dam' good is it?'

'I don't know.'

'Nor does anybody else. Well, now that he's gone, you can give me that money. Did old Tuppy cough up cheerfully?'

'Blithely.'

'I knew it,' said Ukridge, deeply moved, 'I knew it. A good fellow. One of the best. I've always liked Tuppy. A man you can rely on. Some day, when I get going on a big scale, he shall have this back a thousand-fold. I'm glad you brought small notes.'

'Why?'

'I want to scatter 'em about on the table in front of this Nickerson blighter.'

'Is this where he lives?'

We had come to a red-roofed house, set back from the road amidst trees. Ukridge wielded the knocker forcefully.

'Tell Mr Nickerson,' he said to the maid, 'that Mr Ukridge has called and would like a word.'

About the demeanour of the man who presently entered the room into which we had been shown there was that subtle but well-marked something which stamps your creditor all the world over. Mr Nickerson was a man of medium height, almost completely surrounded by whiskers, and through the shrubbery he gazed at Ukridge with frozen eyes, shooting out waves of deleterious animal magnetism. You could see at a glance that he was not fond of Ukridge. Take him for all in all, Mr Nickerson looked like one of the less amiable prophets of the Old Testament about to interview the captive monarch of the Amalekites.

'Well?' he said, and I have never heard the word spoken in a more forbidding manner.

'I've come about the rent.'

'Ah!' said Mr Nickerson, guardedly.

'To pay it,' said Ukridge.

'To pay it!' ejaculated Mr Nickerson, incredulously.

'Here!' said Ukridge, and with a superb gesture flung money on the table.

I understood now why the massive-minded man had

wanted small notes. They made a brave display. There was a light breeze blowing in through the open window, and so musical a rustling did it set up as it played about the heaped-up wealth that Mr Nickerson's austerity seemed to vanish like breath off a razor-blade. For a moment a dazed look came into his eyes and he swayed slightly; then, as he started to gather up the money, he took on the benevolent air of a bishop blessing pilgrims. As far as Mr Nickerson was concerned, the sun was up.

'Why, thank you, Mr Ukridge, I'm sure,' he said. 'Thank you very much. No hard feelings, I trust?'

'Not on my side, old horse,' responded Ukridge, affably. 'Business is business.'

'Exactly.'

'Well, I may as well take those dogs now,' said Ukridge, helping himself to a cigar from a box which he had just discovered on the mantelpiece and putting a couple more in his pocket in the friendliest way. 'The sooner they're back with me, the better. They've lost a day's education as it is.'

'Why, certainly, Mr Ukridge; certainly. They are in the shed at the bottom of the garden. I will get them for you at once.'

He retreated through the door, babbling ingratiatingly.

'Amazing how fond these blokes are of money,' sighed Ukridge. 'It's a thing I don't like to see. Sordid, I call it. That blighter's eyes were gleaming, positively gleaming, laddie, as he scooped up the stuff. Good cigars these,' he added, pocketing three more.

There was a faltering footstep outside, and Mr Nickerson re-entered the room. The man appeared to have something on his mind. A glassy look was in his whisker-bordered eyes, and his mouth, though it was not easy to see it through the jungle, seemed to me to be sagging mournfully. He resembled a minor prophet who has been hit behind the ear with a stuffed eel-skin.

'Mr Ukridge!'

'Hallo?'

'The – the little dogs!'

'Well?'

'The little dogs!'

'What about them?'

'They have gone!'

'Gone?'

'Run away!'

'Run away? How the devil could they run away?'

'There seems to have been a loose board at the back of the shed. The little dogs must have wriggled through. There is no trace of them to be found.'

Ukridge flung up his arms despairingly. He swelled like a captive balloon. His pince-nez rocked on his nose, his mackintosh flapped menacingly, and his collar sprang off its stud. He brought his fist down with a crash on the table.

'Upon my Sam!'

'I am extremely sorry——'

'Upon my Sam!' cried Ukridge. 'It's hard. It's pretty hard. I come down here to inaugurate a great business,

46

which would eventually have brought trade and prosperity to the whole neighbourhood, and I have hardly had time to turn round and attend to the preliminary details of the enterprise when this man comes and sneaks my dogs. And now he tells me with a light laugh—'

'Mr Ukridge, I assure you—'

'Tells me with a light laugh that they've gone. Gone! Gone where? Why, dash it, they may be all over the county. A fat chance I've got of ever seeing them again. Six valuable Pekingese, already educated practically to the stage where they could have been sold at an enormous profit—'

Mr Nickerson was fumbling guiltily, and now he produced from his pocket a crumpled wad of notes, which he thrust agitatedly upon Ukridge, who waved them away with loathing.

'This gentleman,' boomed Ukridge, indicating me with a sweeping gesture, 'happens to be a lawyer. It is extremely lucky that he chanced to come down today to pay me a visit. Have you followed the proceedings closely?'

I said I had followed them very closely.

'Is it your opinion that an action will lie?'

I said it seemed highly probable, and this expert ruling appeared to put the final touch on Mr Nickerson's collapse. Almost tearfully he urged the notes on Ukridge.

'What's this?' said Ukridge, loftily.

'I – I thought, Mr Ukridge, that, if it were agreeable

to you, you might consent to take your money back, and – and consider the episode closed.'

Ukridge turned to me with raised eyebrows.

'Ha!' he cried. 'Ha, ha!'

'Ha, ha!' I chorused, dutifully.

'He thinks that he can close the episode by giving me my money back. Isn't that rich?'

'Fruity,' I agreed.

'Those dogs were worth hundreds of pounds, and he thinks he can square me with a rotten twenty. Would you have believed it if you hadn't heard it with your own ears, old horse?'

'Never!'

'I'll tell you what I'll do,' said Ukridge, after thought. 'I'll take this money.' Mr Nickerson thanked him. 'And there are one or two trifling accounts which want settling with some of the local tradesmen. You will square those—'

'Certainly, Mr Ukridge, certainly.'

'And after that – well, I'll have to think it over. If I decide to institute proceedings my lawyer will communicate with you in due course.'

And we left the wretched man, cowering despicably behind his whiskers.

It seemed to me, as we passed down the tree-shaded lane and out into the white glare of the road, that Ukridge was bearing himself in his hour of disaster with a rather admirable fortitude. His stock-in-trade, the life-blood of his enterprise, was scattered all over Kent, probably never to return, and all that he had to show on the other side of the balance-sheet was the cancelling of a few weeks' back rent and the paying-off of Gooch, the grocer, and his friends. It was a situation which might well have crushed the spirit of an ordinary man, but Ukridge seemed by no means dejected. Jaunty, rather. His eyes shone behind their pince-nez and he whistled a rollicking air. When presently he began to sing, I felt that it was time to create a diversion.

'What are you going to do?' I asked.

'Who, me?' said Ukridge, buoyantly. 'Oh, I'm coming back to town on the next train. You don't mind hoofing it to the next station, do you? It's only five miles. It might be a trifle risky to start from Sheep's Cray.'

'Why risky?'

'Because of the dogs, of course.'

'Dogs?'

Ukridge hummed a gay strain.

'Oh, yes. I forgot to tell you about that. I've got 'em.'

'What?'

'Yes. I went out late last night and pinched them out of the shed.' He chuckled amusedly. 'Perfectly simple. Only needed a clear, level head. I borrowed a dead cat and tied a string to it, legged it to old Nickerson's garden after dark, dug a board out of the back of the shed, and shoved my head down and chirruped. The dogs came trickling out, and I hared off, towing old Colonel Cat on his string. Great run while it lasted, laddie.

Hounds picked up the scent right away and started off in a bunch at fifty miles an hour. Cat and I doing a steady fifty-five. Thought every minute old Nickerson would hear and start blazing away with a gun, but nothing happened. I led the pack across country for a run of twenty minutes without a check, parked the dogs in my sitting-room, and so to bed. Took it out of me, by gosh! Not so young as I was.'

I was silent for a moment, conscious of a feeling almost of reverence. This man was undoubtedly spacious. There had always been something about Ukridge that dulled the moral sense.

'Well,' I said at length, 'you've certainly got vision.'

'Yes?' said Ukridge, gratified.

'*And* the big, broad, flexible outlook.'

'Got to, laddie, nowadays. The foundation of a successful business career.'

'And what's the next move?'

We were drawing near to the White Cottage. It stood and broiled in the sunlight, and I hoped that there might be something cool to drink inside it. The window of the sitting-room was open, and through it came the yapping of Pekingese.

'Oh, I shall find another cottage somewhere else,' said Ukridge, eyeing his little home with a certain sentimentality. 'That won't be hard. Lots of cottages all over the place. And then I shall buckle down to serious work. You'll be astounded at the progress I've made already. In a minute I'll show you what those dogs can do.'

'They can bark all right.'

'Yes. They seem excited about something. You know, laddie, I've had a great idea. When I saw you at your rooms my scheme was to specialize in performing dogs for the music-halls – what you might call professional dogs. But I've been thinking it over, and now I don't see why I shouldn't go in for developing amateur talent as well. Say you have a dog – Fido, the household pet – and you think it would brighten the home if he could do a few tricks from time to time. Well, you're a busy man, you haven't the time to give up to teaching him. So you just tie a label to his collar and ship him off for a month to the Ukridge Dog College, and back he comes, thoroughly educated. No trouble, no worry, easy terms. Upon my Sam, I'm not sure there isn't more money in the amateur branch than in the professional. I don't see why eventually dog owners shouldn't send their dogs to me as a regular thing, just as they send their sons to Eton and Winchester. My golly! this idea's beginning to develop. I'll tell you what – how would it be to issue special collars to all dogs which have graduated from my college? Something distinctive which everybody would recognize. See what I mean? Sort of badge of honour. Fellow with a dog entitled to wear the Ukridge collar would be in a position to look down on the bloke whose dog hadn't got one. Gradually it would get so that anybody in a decent social position would be ashamed to be seen out with a non-Ukridge dog. The thing would become a landslide.

Dogs would pour in from all corners of the country. More work than I could handle. Have to start branches. The scheme's colossal. Millions in it, my boy! Millions!' He paused with his fingers on the handle of the front door. 'Of course,' he went on, 'just at present it's no good blinking the fact that I'm hampered and handicapped by lack of funds and can only approach the thing on a small scale. What it amounts to, laddie, is that somehow or other I've got to get capital.'

It seemed the moment to spring the glad news.

'I promised him I wouldn't mention it,' I said, 'for fear it might lead to disappointment, but as a matter of fact George Tupper is trying to raise some capital for you. I left him last night starting out to get it.'

'George Tupper!' – Ukridge's eyes dimmed with a not unmanly emotion – 'George Tupper! By Gad, that fellow is the salt of the earth. Good, loyal fellow! A true friend. A man you can rely on. Upon my Sam, if there were more fellows about like old Tuppy, there wouldn't be all this modern pessimism and unrest. Did he seem to have any idea where he could raise a bit of capital for me?'

'Yes. He went round to tell your aunt about your coming down here to train those Pekes, and – What's the matter?'

A fearful change had come over Ukridge's jubilant front. His eyes bulged, his jaw sagged. With the addition of a few feet of grey whiskers he would have looked exactly like the recent Mr Nickerson.

'My aunt?' he mumbled, swaying on the door-handle.

'Yes. What's the matter? He thought, if he told her all about it, she might relent and rally round.'

The sigh of a gallant fighter at the end of his strength forced its way up from Ukridge's mackintosh-covered bosom.

'Of all the dashed, infernal, officious, meddling, muddling, fat-headed, interfering asses,' he said, wanly, 'George Tupper is the worst.'

'What do you mean?'

'The man oughtn't to be at large. He's a public menace.'

'But—'

'Those dogs *belong* to my aunt. I pinched them when she chucked me out!'

Inside the cottage the Pekingese were still yapping industriously.

'Upon my Sam,' said Ukridge, 'it's a little hard.'

I think he would have said more, but at this point a voice spoke with a sudden and awful abruptness from the interior of the cottage. It was a woman's voice, a quiet, steely voice, a voice, it seemed to me, that suggested cold eyes, a beaky nose, and hair like gun-metal.

'Stanley!'

That was all it said, but it was enough. Ukridge's eye met mine in a wild surmise. He seemed to shrink into his mackintosh like a snail surprised while eating lettuce.

'Stanley!'

'Yes. Aunt Julia?' quavered Ukridge.

'Come here. I wish to speak to you.'

'Yes, Aunt Julia.'

I sidled out into the road. Inside the cottage the yapping of the Pekingese had become quite hysterical. I found myself trotting, and then – though it was a warm day – running quite rapidly. I could have stayed if I had wanted to, but somehow I did not want to. Something seemed to tell me that on this holy domestic scene I should be an intruder.

What it was that gave me that impression I do not know – probably vision or the big, broad, flexible outlook.

'Half a minute, laddie,' said Ukridge. And, gripping my arm, he brought me to a halt on the outskirts of the little crowd which had collected about the church door.

It was a crowd such as may be seen any morning during the London mating-season outside any of the churches which nestle in the quiet squares between Hyde Park and the King's Road, Chelsea.

It consisted of five women of cooklike aspect, four nursemaids, half a dozen men of the non-producing class who had torn themselves away for the moment from their normal task of propping up the wall of the Bunch of Grapes public-house on the corner, a coster-monger with a barrow of vegetables, divers small boys, eleven dogs, and two or three purposeful-looking young fellows with cameras slung over their shoulders. It was plain that a wedding was in progress – and, arguing from the presence of the camera-men and the line of smart motor-cars along the kerb, a fairly fashionable wedding. What was not plain – to me – was why Ukridge, sternest of bachelors, had desired to add himself to the spectators.

'What,' I inquired, 'is the thought behind this? Why are we interrupting our walk to attend the obsequies of some perfect stranger?'

Ukridge did not reply for a moment. He seemed plunged in thought. Then he uttered a hollow, mirthless laugh — a dreadful sound like the last gargle of a dying moose.

'Perfect stranger, my number eleven foot!' he responded, in his coarse way. 'Do you know who it is who's getting hitched up in there?'

'Who?'

'Teddy Weeks.'

'Teddy Weeks? Teddy Weeks? Good Lord!' I exclaimed. 'Not really?'

And five years rolled away.

It was at Barolini's Italian restaurant in Beak Street that Ukridge evolved his great scheme. Barolini's was a favourite resort of our little group of earnest strugglers in the days when the philanthropic restaurateurs of Soho used to supply four courses and coffee for a shilling and sixpence; and there were present that night, besides Ukridge and myself, the following men-about-town: Teddy Weeks, the actor, fresh from a six-weeks' tour with the Number Three 'Only a Shop-Girl' Company; Victor Beamish, the artist, the man who drew that picture of the O-So-Eesi Piano-Player in the advertisement pages of the *Piccadilly Magazine*; Bertram

Fox, author of *Ashes of Remorse*, and other unproduced
motion-picture scenarios; and Robert Dunhill, who,
being employed at a salary of eighty pounds per annum
by the New Asiatic Bank, represented the sober, hard-
headed commercial element. As usual, Teddy Weeks
had collared the conversation, and was telling us once
again how good he was and how hardly treated by a
malignant fate.

There is no need to describe Teddy Weeks. Under
another and a more euphonious name he has long since
made his personal appearance dreadfully familiar to all
who read the illustrated weekly papers. He was then, as
now, a sickeningly handsome young man, possessing
precisely the same melting eyes, mobile mouth, and
corrugated hair so esteemed by the theatre-going public
today. And yet, at this period of his career he was wast-
ing himself on minor touring companies of the kind
which open at Barrow-in-Furness and jump to Bootle
for the second half of the week. He attributed this, as
Ukridge was so apt to attribute his own difficulties, to
lack of capital.

'I have everything,' he said, querulously, emphasizing
his remarks with a coffee-spoon. 'Looks, talent, personality, a beautiful speaking voice – everything. All I
need is a chance. And I can't get that because I have no
clothes fit to wear. These managers are all the same,
they never look below the surface, they never bother to
find out if a man has genius. All they go by are his
clothes. If I could afford to buy a couple of suits from a

Cork Street tailor, if I could have my boots made to order by Moykoff instead of getting them ready-made and second-hand at Moses Brothers', if I could once contrive to own a decent hat, a really good pair of spats, and a gold cigarette-case, all at the same time, I could walk into any manager's office in London and sign up for a West-end production tomorrow.'

It was at this point that Freddie Lunt came in. Freddie, like Robert Dunhill, was a financial magnate in the making and an assiduous frequenter of Barolini's; and it suddenly occurred to us that a considerable time had passed since we had last seen him in the place. We inquired the reason for this aloofness.

'I've been in bed,' said Freddie, 'for over a fortnight.'

The statement incurred Ukridge's stern disapproval. That great man made a practice of never rising before noon, and on one occasion, when a carelessly-thrown match had burned a hole in his only pair of trousers, had gone so far as to remain between the sheets for forty-eight hours; but sloth on so majestic a scale as this shocked him.

'Lazy young devil,' he commented severely. 'Letting the golden hours of youth slip by like that when you ought to have been bustling about and making a name for yourself.'

Freddie protested himself wronged by the imputation.

'I had an accident,' he explained. 'Fell off my bicycle and sprained an ankle.'

'Tough luck,' was our verdict.

'Oh, I don't know,' said Freddie. 'It wasn't bad fun getting a rest. And of course there was the fiver.'

'What fiver?'

'I got a fiver from the *Weekly Cyclist* for getting my ankle sprained.'

'You — *what*?' cried Ukridge, profoundly stirred — as ever — by a tale of easy money. 'Do you mean to sit there and tell me that some dashed paper paid you five quid simply because you sprained your ankle? Pull yourself together, old horse. Things like that don't happen.'

'It's quite true.'

'Can you show me the fiver?'

'No; because if I did you would try to borrow it.'

Ukridge ignored this slur in dignified silence.

'Would they pay a fiver to *anyone* who sprained his ankle?' he asked, sticking to the main point.

'Yes. If he was a subscriber.'

'I knew there was a catch in it,' said Ukridge, moodily.

'Lots of weekly papers are starting this wheeze,' proceeded Freddie. 'You pay a year's subscription and that entitles you to accident insurance.'

We were interested. This was in the days before every daily paper in London was competing madly against its rivals in the matter of insurance and offering princely bribes to the citizens to make a fortune by breaking their necks. Nowadays papers are paying as high as two thousand pounds for a genuine corpse and five pounds a week for a mere dislocated spine; but at that time the idea was new and it had an attractive appeal.

'How many of these rags are doing this?' asked Ukridge. You could tell from the gleam in his eyes that that great brain was whirring like a dynamo. 'As many as ten?'

'Yes, I should think so. Quite ten.'

'Then a fellow who subscribed to them all and then sprained his ankle would get fifty quid?' said Ukridge, reasoning acutely.

'More if the injury was more serious,' said Freddie, the expert. 'They have a regular tariff. So much for a broken arm, so much for a broken leg, and so forth.'

Ukridge's collar leaped off its stud and his pince-nez wobbled drunkenly as he turned to us.

'How much money can you blokes raise?' he demanded.

'What do you want it for?' asked Robert Dunhill, with a banker's caution.

'My dear old horse, can't you see? Why, my gosh, I've got the idea of the century. Upon my Sam, this is the giltest-edged scheme that was ever hatched. We'll get together enough money and take out a year's subscription for every one of these dashed papers.'

'What's the good of that?' said Dunhill, coldly unenthusiastic.

They train bank clerks to stifle emotion, so that they will be able to refuse overdrafts when they become managers. 'The odds are we should none of us have an accident of any kind, and then the money would be chucked away.'

'Good heavens, ass,' snorted Ukridge, 'you don't suppose I'm suggesting that we should leave it to chance, do you? Listen! Here's the scheme. We take out subscriptions for all these papers, then we draw lots, and the fellow who gets the fatal card or whatever it is goes out and breaks his leg and draws the loot, and we split it up between us and live on it in luxury. It ought to run into hundreds of pounds.'

A long silence followed. Then Dunhill spoke again. His was a solid rather than a nimble mind.

'Suppose he couldn't break his leg?'

'My gosh!' cried Ukridge, exasperated. 'Here we are in the twentieth century, with every resource of modern civilization at our disposal, with opportunities for getting our legs broken opening about us on every side – and you ask a silly question like that! Of course he could break his leg. Any ass can break a leg. It's a little hard! We're all infernally broke – personally, unless Freddie can lend me a bit of that fiver till Saturday, I'm going to have a difficult job pulling through. We all need money like the dickens, and yet, when I point out this marvellous scheme for collecting a bit, instead of fawning on me for my ready intelligence you sit and make objections. It isn't the right spirit. It isn't the spirit that wins.'

'If you're as hard up as that,' objected Dunhill, 'how are you going to put in your share of the pool?'

A pained, almost a stunned, look came into Ukridge's eyes. He gazed at Dunhill through his lop-sided pince-nez as one who speculates as to whether his hearing has deceived him.

'Me?' he cried. 'Me? I like that! Upon my Sam, that's rich! Why, damme, if there's any justice in the world, if there's a spark of decency and good feeling in your bally bosoms, I should think you would let me in free for suggesting the idea. It's a little hard! I supply the brains and you want me to cough up cash as well. My gosh, I didn't expect this. This hurts me, by George! If anybody had told me that an old pal would—'

'Oh, all right,' said Robert Dunhill. 'All right, all right, all right. But I'll tell you one thing. If you draw the lot it'll be the happiest day of my life.'

'I shan't,' said Ukridge. 'Something tells me that I shan't.'

Nor did he. When, in a solemn silence broken only by the sound of a distant waiter quarrelling with the cook down a speaking-tube, we had completed the drawing, the man of destiny was Teddy Weeks.

I suppose that even in the springtime of Youth, when broken limbs seem a lighter matter than they become later in life, it can never be an unmixedly agreeable thing to have to go out into the public high-ways and try to make an accident happen to one. In such circumstances the reflection that you are thereby benefiting your friends brings but slight balm. To Teddy Weeks it appeared to bring no balm at all. That he was experiencing a certain disinclination to sacrifice himself for the public good became more and more evident as the days went by and found him still intact. Ukridge, when he called upon me to discuss the matter, was visibly perturbed. He sank into a chair beside the table at which I was beginning my modest morning meal, and, having drunk half my coffee, sighed deeply.

'Upon my Sam,' he moaned, 'it's a little disheartening. I strain my brain to think up schemes for getting us all a bit of money just at the moment when we are all needing it most, and when I hit on what is probably the simplest and yet ripest notion of our time, this blighter Weeks goes and lets me down by shirking his plain duty. It's just my luck that a fellow like that should have drawn the lot. And the worst of it is, laddie, that, now we've started with him, we've got to keep on. We can't possibly raise enough money to pay yearly subscriptions for anybody else. It's Weeks or nobody.'

'I suppose we must give him time.'

'That's what he says,' grunted Ukridge, morosely, helping himself to toast. 'He says he doesn't know how to start about it. To listen to him, you'd think that going and having a trifling accident was the sort of delicate and intricate job that required years of study and special preparation. Why, a child of six could do it on his head at five minutes' notice. The man's so infernally particular. You make helpful suggestions, and instead of accepting them in a broad, reasonable spirit of cooperation he comes back at you every time with some frivolous objection. He's so dashed fastidious. When we were out last night, we came on a couple of navvies scrapping. Good hefty fellows, either of them capable of putting him in hospital for a month. I told him to jump in and start separating them, and he said no; it was a private dispute which was none of his business, and he didn't feel justified in interfering. Finicky, I call it. I tell you, laddie, this blighter is a broken reed. He has got cold feet. We did wrong to let him into the drawing at all. We might have known that a fellow like that would never give results. No conscience. No sense of *esprit de corps*. No notion of putting himself out to the most trifling extent for the benefit of the community. Haven't you any more marmalade, laddie?'

'I have not.'

'Then I'll be going,' said Ukridge, moodily. 'I suppose,' he added, pausing at the door, 'you couldn't lend me five bob?'

'How did you guess?'

'Then I'll tell you what,' said Ukridge, ever fair and reasonable; 'you can stand me dinner tonight.' He seemed cheered up for the moment by this happy compromise, but gloom descended on him again. His face clouded. 'When I think,' he said, 'of all the money that's locked up in that poor faint-hearted fish, just waiting to be released, I could sob. Sob, laddie, like a little child. I never liked that man — he has a bad eye and waves his hair. Never trust a man who waves his hair, old horse.'

Ukridge's pessimism was not confined to himself. By the end of a fortnight, nothing having happened to Teddy Weeks worse than a slight cold which he shook off in a couple of days, the general consensus of opinion among his apprehensive colleagues in the Syndicate was that the situation had become desperate. There were no signs whatever of any return on the vast capital which we had laid out, and meanwhile meals had to be bought, landladies paid, and a reasonable supply of tobacco acquired. It was a melancholy task in these circumstances to read one's paper of a morning.

All over the inhabited globe, so the well-informed sheet gave one to understand, every kind of accident was happening every day to practically everybody in existence except Teddy Weeks. Farmers in Minnesota were getting mixed up with reaping-machines, peasants in India were being bisected by crocodiles; iron girders from skyscrapers were falling hourly on the heads of citizens in every town from Philadelphia to San Francisco; and the only people who were not down with ptomaine poisoning were those who had walked over cliffs, driven motors into walls, tripped over manholes, or assumed on too slight evidence that the gun was not loaded. In a crippled world, it seemed, Teddy Weeks walked alone, whole and glowing with health. It was one of those grim, ironical, hopeless, grey, despairful situations which the Russian novelists love to write about, and I could not find it in me to blame Ukridge for taking direct action in this crisis. My only regret was that bad luck caused so excellent a plan to miscarry.

My first intimation that he had been trying to hurry matters on came when he and I were walking along the King's Road one evening, and he drew me into Markham Square, a dismal backwater where he had once had rooms.

'What's the idea?' I asked, for I disliked the place.

'Teddy Weeks lives here,' said Ukridge. 'In my old rooms.' I could not see that this lent any fascination to the place. Every day and in every way I was feeling sorrier and sorrier that I had been foolish enough to put money which I could ill spare into a venture which had all the earmarks of a wash-out, and my sentiments towards Teddy Weeks were cold and hostile.

'I want to inquire after him.'

'Inquire after him? Why?'

'Well, the fact is, laddie, I have an idea that he has been bitten by a dog.'

'What makes you think that?'

'Oh, I don't know,' said Ukridge, dreamily. 'I've just got the idea. You know how one gets ideas.'

The mere contemplation of this beautiful event was so inspiring that for a while it held me silent. In each of the ten journals in which we had invested dog-bites were specifically recommended as things which every subscriber ought to have. They came about half-way up the list of lucrative accidents, inferior to a broken rib or a fractured fibula, but better value than an ingrowing

toe-nail. I was gloating happily over the picture con-
jured up by Ukridge's words when an exclamation
brought me back with a start to the realities of life. A
revolting sight met my eyes. Down the street came
ambling the familiar figure of Teddy Weeks, and one
glance at his elegant person was enough to tell us that
our hopes had been built on sand. Not even a toy
Pomeranian had chewed this man.

'Hallo, you fellows!' said Teddy Weeks.

'Hallo!' we responded, dully.

'Can't stop,' said Teddy Weeks. 'I've got to fetch a
doctor.'

'A doctor?'

'Yes. Poor Victor Beamish. He's been bitten by
a dog.'

Ukridge and I exchanged weary glances. It seemed
as if Fate was going out of its way to have sport with us.
What was the good of a dog biting Victor Beamish?
What was the good of a hundred dogs biting Victor
Beamish? A dog-bitten Victor Beamish had no market
value whatever.

'You know that fierce brute that belongs to my landlady,' said Teddy Weeks. 'The one that always dashes
out into the area and barks at people who come to the
front door.' I remembered. A large mongrel with wild
eyes and flashing fangs, badly in need of a haircut. I had
encountered it once in the street, when visiting
Ukridge, and only the presence of the latter, who knew
it well and to whom all dogs were as brothers, had

saved me from the doom of Victor Beamish. 'Some-how or other he got into my bedroom this evening. He was waiting there when I came home. I had brought Beamish back with me, and the animal pinned him by the leg the moment I opened the door.'

'Why didn't he pin you?' asked Ukridge, aggrieved.

'What I can't make out,' said Teddy Weeks, 'is how on earth the brute came to be in my room. Somebody must have put him there. The whole thing is very mysterious.'

'Why didn't he pin you?' demanded Ukridge again.

'Oh, I managed to climb on to the top of the ward-robe while he was biting Beamish,' said Teddy Weeks. 'And then the landlady came and took him away. But I can't stop here talking. I must go and get that doctor.'

We gazed after him in silence as he tripped down the street. We noted the careful manner in which he paused at the corner to eye the traffic before crossing the road, the wary way in which he drew back to allow a truck to rattle past.

'You heard that?' said Ukridge, tensely. 'He climbed on to the top of the wardrobe!'

'Yes.'

'And you saw the way he dodged that excellent truck?'

'Yes.'

'Something's got to be done,' said Ukridge, firmly. 'The man has got to be awakened to a sense of his responsibilities.'

Next day a deputation waited on Teddy Weeks.

Ukridge was our spokesman, and he came to the point with admirable directness.

'How about it?' asked Ukridge.

'How about what?' replied Teddy Weeks, nervously, avoiding his accusing eye.

'When do we get action?'

'Oh, you mean that accident business?'

'Yes.'

'I've been thinking about that,' said Teddy Weeks.

Ukridge drew the mackintosh which he wore indoors and out of doors in all weathers more closely around him. There was in the action something suggestive of a member of the Roman Senate about to denounce an enemy of the State. In just such a manner must Cicero have swished his toga as he took a deep breath preparatory to assailing Clodius. He toyed for a moment with the ginger-beer wire which held his pince-nez in place, and endeavoured without success to button his collar at the back. In moments of emotion Ukridge's collar always took on a sort of temperamental jumpiness which no stud could restrain.

'And about time you *were* thinking about it,' he boomed, sternly.

We shifted appreciatively in our seats, all except Victor Beamish, who had declined a chair and was standing by the mantelpiece. 'Upon my Sam, it's about time you were thinking about it. Do you realize that we've invested an enormous sum of money in you on the distinct understanding that we could rely on you to do your duty and get immediate results? Are we to be forced to the conclusion that you are so yellow and few in the pod as to want to evade your honourable obligations? We thought better of you, Weeks. Upon my Sam, we thought better of you. We took you for a two-fisted, enterprising, big-souled, one-hundred-per-cent he-man who would stand by his friends to the finish.'

'Yes, but—'

'Any bloke with a sense of loyalty and an appreciation of what it meant to the rest of us would have rushed out and found some means of fulfilling his duty long ago. You don't even grasp at the opportunities that come your way. Only yesterday I saw you draw back when a single step into the road would have had a truck bumping into you.'

'Well, it's not so easy to let a truck bump into you.'

'Nonsense. It only requires a little ordinary resolution. Use your imagination, man. Try to think that a child has fallen down in the street – a little golden-haired child,' said Ukridge, deeply affected. 'And a dashed great cab or something comes rolling up. The kid's mother is standing on the pavement, helpless, her hands clasped in agony. "Dammit," she cries, "will no one save my darling?" "Yes, by George," you shout, "*I* will." And out you jump and the thing's over in half a second. I don't know what you're making such a fuss about.'

'Yes, but—' said Teddy Weeks.

'I'm told, what's more, it isn't a bit painful. A sort of dull shock, that's all.'

'Who told you that?'

'I forget. Someone.'

'Well, you can tell him from me that he's an ass,' said Teddy Weeks, with asperity.

'All right. If you object to being run over by a truck there are lots of other ways. But, upon my Sam, it's pretty hopeless suggesting them. You seem to have no enterprise at all. Yesterday, after I went to all the trouble to put a dog in your room, a dog which would have done all the work for you – all you had to do was stand still and let him use his own judgement – what happened? You climbed on to—'

Victor Beamish interrupted, speaking in a voice husky with emotion.

'Was it you who put that damned dog in the room?'

'Eh?' said Ukridge. 'Why, yes. But we can have a good talk about all that later on,' he proceeded, hastily. 'The point at the moment is how the dickens we're going to persuade this poor worm to collect our insurance money for us. Why, damme, I should have thought you would have—'

'All I can say—' began Victor Beamish, heatedly.

'Yes, yes,' said Ukridge; 'some other time. Must stick to business now, laddie. I was saying,' he resumed, 'that I should have thought you would have been as keen as mustard to put the job through for your own sake. You're always beefing that you haven't any clothes to impress managers with. Think of all you can buy with your share of the swag once you have summoned up a little ordinary determination and seen the thing through. Think of the suits, the boots, the hats, the spats. You're always talking about your dashed career, and how all you need to land you in a West-end production is good clothes. Well, here's your chance to get them.'

His eloquence was not wasted. A wistful look came into Teddy Weeks's eye, such a look as must have come into the eye of Moses on the summit of Pisgah. He breathed heavily! You could see that the man was mentally walking along Cork Street, weighing the merits of one famous tailor against another.

'I'll tell you what I'll do,' he said, suddenly. 'It's no use asking me to put this thing through in cold blood. I simply can't do it. I haven't the nerve. But if you fellows will give me a dinner tonight with lots of champagne I think it will key me up to it.'

A heavy silence fell upon the room. Champagne! The word was like a knell.

'How on earth are we going to afford champagne?' said Victor Beamish.

'Well, there it is,' said Teddy Weeks. 'Take it or leave it.'

'Gentlemen,' said Ukridge, 'it would seem that the company requires more capital. How about it, old horses? Let's get together in a frank, business-like, cards-on-the-table spirit, and see what can be done. I can raise ten bob.'

'What!' cried the entire assembled company, amazed. 'How?'

'I'll pawn a banjo.'

'You haven't got a banjo.'

'No, but George Tupper has, and I know where he keeps it.'

Started in this spirited way, the subscriptions came pouring in. I contributed a cigarette-case, Bertram Fox thought his landlady would let him owe for another week, Robert Dunhill had an uncle in Kensington who, he fancied, if tactfully approached, would be good for a quid, and Victor Beamish said that if the advertisement-manager of the O-So-Eesi Piano-Player was churlish enough to refuse an advance of five shillings against future work he misjudged him sadly. Within a few minutes, in short, the Lightning Drive had produced the impressive total of two pounds six shillings, and we asked Teddy Weeks if he thought that he could get adequately keyed up within the limits of that sum.

'I'll try,' said Teddy Weeks.

So, not unmindful of the fact that that excellent hostelry supplied champagne at eight shillings the quart bottle, we fixed the meeting for seven o'clock at Barolini's.

Considered as a social affair, Teddy Weeks's keying-up dinner was not a success. Almost from the start I think we all found it trying. It was not so much the fact that he was drinking deeply of Barolini's eight-shilling champagne while we, from lack of funds, were compelled to confine ourselves to meaner beverages; what really marred the pleasantness of the function was the extraordinary effect the stuff had on Teddy. What was actually in the champagne supplied to Barolini and purveyed by him to the public, such as were reckless enough to drink it, at eight shillings the bottle, remains a secret between its maker and his Maker; but three glasses of it were enough to convert Teddy Weeks from a mild and rather oily young man into a truculent swashbuckler.

He quarrelled with us all. With the soup he was tilting at Victor Beamish's theories of Art; the fish found him ridiculing Bertram Fox's views on the future of the motion-picture; and by the time the leg of chicken with dandelion salad arrived – or, as some held, string salad – opinions varied on this point – the hell-brew had so wrought on him that he had begun to lecture Ukridge on his mis-spent life and was urging him in accents audible across the street to go out and get a job and thus acquire sufficient self-respect to enable him to look himself in the face in a mirror without wincing. Not, added Teddy Weeks, with what we all thought uncalled-for offensiveness, that any amount of self-respect was likely to do that. Having said which, he called imperiously for another eight bobs'-worth.

We gazed at one another wanly. However excellent the end towards which all this was tending, there was no denying that it was hard to bear. But policy kept us silent. We recognized that this was Teddy Weeks's evening and that he must be humoured. Victor

Beamish said meekly that Teddy had cleared up a lot of points which had been troubling him for a long time. Bertram Fox agreed that there was much in what Teddy had said about the future of the close-up. And even Ukridge, though his haughty soul was seared to its foundations by the latter's personal remarks, promised to take his homily to heart and act upon it at the earliest possible moment.

'You'd better!' said Teddy Weeks, belligerently, biting off the end of one of Barolini's best cigars. 'And there's another thing – don't let me hear of your coming and sneaking people's socks again.'

'Very well, laddie,' said Ukridge, humbly.

'If there is one person in the world that I despise,' said Teddy, bending a red-eyed gaze on the offender, 'it's a snock-seeker – a seek-snocker – a – well, you know what I mean.'

We hastened to assure him that we knew what he meant and he relapsed into a lengthy stupor, from which he emerged three-quarters of an hour later to announce that he didn't know what we intended to do, but that he was going. We said that we were going too, and we paid the bill and did so.

Teddy Weeks's indignation on discovering us gathered about him upon the pavement outside the restaurant was intense, and he expressed it freely. Among other things, he said – which was not true – that he had a reputation to keep up in Soho.

'It's all right, Teddy, old horse,' said Ukridge,

soothingly. 'We just thought you would like to have all your old pals round you when you did it.'

'Did it? Did what?'

'Why, had the accident.'

Teddy Weeks glared at him truculently. Then his mood seemed to change abruptly, and he burst into a loud and hearty laugh.

'Well, of all the silly ideas!' he cried, amusedly. 'I'm not going to have an accident. You don't suppose I ever seriously intended to have an accident, do you? It was just my fun.' Then, with another sudden change of mood, he seemed to become a victim to an acute unhappiness. He stroked Ukridge's arm affectionately, and a tear rolled down his cheek. 'Just my fun,' he repeated. 'You don't mind my fun, do you?' he asked, pleadingly. 'You like my fun, don't you? All my fun. Never meant to have an accident at all. Just wanted dinner.' The gay humour of it all overcame his sorrow once more. 'Funniest thing ever heard,' he said cordially. 'Didn't want accident, wanted dinner. Dinner daxident, danner dixident,' he added, driving home his point. 'Well, good night all,' he said, cheerily. And, stepping off the kerb on to a banana-skin, was instantly knocked ten feet by a passing lorry.

'Two ribs and an arm,' said the doctor five minutes later, superintending the removal proceedings. 'Gently with that stretcher.'

It was two weeks before we were informed by the authorities of Charing Cross Hospital that the patient was in a condition to receive visitors. A whip-round secured the price of a basket of fruit, and Ukridge and I were deputed by the shareholders to deliver it with their compliments and kind inquiries.

'Hallo!' we said in a hushed, bedside manner when finally admitted to his presence.

'Sit down, gentlemen,' replied the invalid.

I must confess even in that first moment to having experienced a slight feeling of surprise. It was not like Teddy Weeks to call us gentlemen. Ukridge, however, seemed to notice nothing amiss.

'Well, well, well,' he said, buoyantly. 'And how are you, laddie? We've brought you a few fragments of fruit.'

'I am getting along capitally,' replied Teddy Weeks, still in that odd precise way which had made his opening words strike me as curious. 'And I should like to say that in my opinion England has reason to be proud of the alertness and enterprise of her great journals. The excellence of their reading-matter, the ingenuity of their various competitions, and, above all, the go-ahead spirit which has resulted in this accident insurance scheme are beyond praise. Have you got that down?' he inquired.

Ukridge and I looked at each other. We had been told that Teddy was practically normal again, but this sounded like delirium.

'Have we got that down, old horse?' asked Ukridge, gently.

Teddy Weeks seemed surprised.

'Aren't you reporters?'

'How do you mean, reporters?'

'I thought you had come from one of these weekly papers that have been paying me insurance money, to interview me,' said Teddy Weeks.

Ukridge and I exchanged another glance. An uneasy glance this time. I think that already a grim foreboding had begun to cast its shadow over us.

'Surely you remember me, Teddy, old horse?' said Ukridge, anxiously.

Teddy Weeks knit his brow, concentrating painfully.

'Why, of course,' he said at last. 'You're Ukridge, aren't you?'

'That's right. Ukridge.'

'Of course. Ukridge.'

'Yes. Ukridge. Funny your forgetting me!'

'Yes,' said Teddy Weeks. 'It's the effect of the shock I got when that thing bowled me over. I must have been struck on the head, I suppose. It has had the effect of rendering my memory rather uncertain. The doctors here are very interested. They say it is a most unusual case. I can remember some things perfectly, but in some ways my memory is a complete blank.'

'Oh, but I say, old horse,' quavered Ukridge. 'I suppose you haven't forgotten about that insurance, have you?'

'Oh, no, I remember that.'

Ukridge breathed a relieved sigh.

'I was a subscriber to a number of weekly papers,'

went on Teddy Weeks. 'They are paying me insurance money now.'

'Yes, yes, old horse,' cried Ukridge. 'But what I mean is you remember the Syndicate, don't you?'

Teddy Weeks raised his eyebrows.

'Syndicate? What Syndicate?'

'Why, when we all got together and put up the money to pay for the subscriptions to these papers and drew lots, to choose which of us should go out and have an accident and collect the money. And you drew it, don't you remember?'

Utter astonishment, and a shocked astonishment at that, spread itself over Teddy Weeks's countenance. The man seemed outraged.

'I certainly remember nothing of the kind,' he said, severely. 'I cannot imagine myself for a moment consenting to become a party to what from your own account would appear to have been a criminal conspiracy to obtain money under false pretences from a number of weekly papers.'

'But, laddie—'

'However,' said Teddy Weeks, 'if there is any truth in this story, no doubt you have documentary evidence to support it.'

Ukridge looked at me. I looked at Ukridge. There was a long silence.

'Shift-ho, old horse?' said Ukridge, sadly. 'No use staying on here.'

'No,' I replied, with equal gloom. 'May as well go.'

'Glad to have seen you,' said Teddy Weeks, 'and thanks for the fruit.'

The next time I saw the man he was coming out of a manager's office in the Haymarket. He had on a new Homburg hat of a delicate pearl grey, spats to match, and a new blue flannel suit, beautifully cut, with an invisible red twill. He was looking jubilant, and, as I passed him, he drew from his pocket a gold cigarette-case.

It was shortly after that, if you remember, that he made a big hit as the juvenile lead in that piece at the Apollo and started on his sensational career as a *matinée* idol.

Inside the church the organ had swelled into the familiar music of the *Wedding March*. A verger came out and opened the doors. The five cooks ceased their reminiscences of other and smarter weddings at which they had participated. The camera-men unshipped their cameras. The costermonger moved his barrow of vegetables a pace forward. A dishevelled and unshaven man at my side uttered a disapproving growl.

'Idle rich!' said the dishevelled man.

Out of the church came a beauteous being, leading attached to his arm another being, somewhat less beauteous.

There was no denying the spectacular effect of Teddy Weeks. He was handsomer than ever. His sleek hair, gorgeously waved, shone in the sun, his eyes were large and bright; his lissom frame, garbed in faultless morning-coat and trousers, was that of an Apollo. But his bride gave the impression that Teddy had married money. They paused in the doorway, and the camera-men became active and fussy.

'Have you got a shilling, laddie?' said Ukridge in a low, level voice.

'Why do you want a shilling?'

'Old horse,' said Ukridge, tensely, 'it is of the utmost vital importance that I have a shilling here and now.'

I passed it over. Ukridge turned to the dishevelled man, and I perceived that he held in his hand a large rich tomato of juicy and over-ripe appearance.

'Would you like to earn a bob?' Ukridge said.

'Would I!' replied the dishevelled man.

Ukridge sank his voice to a hoarse whisper.

The camera-men had finished their preparations. Teddy Weeks, his head thrown back in that gallant way which has endeared him to so many female hearts, was exhibiting his celebrated teeth. The cooks, in undertones, were making adverse comments on the appearance of the bride.

'Now, please,' said one of the camera-men.

Over the heads of the crowd, well and truly aimed, whizzed a large juicy tomato. It burst like a shell full between Teddy Weeks's expressive eyes, obliterating them in scarlet ruin. It spattered Teddy Weeks's collar, it dripped on Teddy Weeks's morning-coat. And the dishevelled man turned abruptly and raced off down the street.

Ukridge grasped my arm. There was a look of deep content in his eyes.

'Shift-ho?' said Ukridge.

Arm-in-arm, we strolled off in the pleasant June sunshine.

PELHAM GRENVILLE WODEHOUSE (always known as 'Plum') wrote more than ninety novels and some three hundred short stories over 73 years. He is widely recognised as the greatest 20th-century writer of humour in the English language.

Perhaps best known for the escapades of Bertie Wooster and Jeeves, Wodehouse also created the world of Blandings Castle, home to Lord Emsworth and his cherished pig, the Empress of Blandings. His stories include gems concerning the irrepressible and disreputable Ukridge; Psmith, the elegant socialist; the ever-so-slightly-unscrupulous Fifth Earl of Ickenham, better known as Uncle Fred; and those related by Mr Mulliner, the charming raconteur of The Angler's Rest, and the Oldest Member at the Golf Club.

In 1936 he was awarded the Mark Twain Prize for 'having made an outstanding and lasting contribution to the happiness of the world'. He was made a Doctor of Letters by Oxford University in 1939 and in 1975, aged 93, he was knighted by Queen Elizabeth II. He died shortly afterwards, on St Valentine's Day.

'Had P. G. Wodehouse's only contribution to literature been Lord Emsworth and Blandings Castle, his place in history would have been assured. Had he written of none but Mike and Psmith, he would be cherished today as the best and brightest of our comic authors. If Jeeves and Wooster had been his solitary theme, still he would be hailed as The Master. If he had given us only Ukridge, or nothing but the recollections of the Mulliner family, or a pure diet of golfing stories, Wodehouse would nonetheless be considered immortal. That he gave us all those and more – so much more – is our good fortune and a testament to the most industrious, prolific and beneficent author ever to have sat down, scratched his head and banged out a sentence.'

Stephen Fry

We hope you have enjoyed this book. With over ninety novels and around 300 short stories to choose from, you may be wondering which Wodehouse to choose next. It is our pleasure to introduce...

UNCLE FRED

Uncle Dynamite

Meet Frederick Altamount Cornwallis Twistleton, Fifth Earl of Ickenham. Better known as Uncle Fred, an old boy of such a sunny and youthful nature that explosions of sweetness and light detonate all around him.

Cocktail Time

Frederick, Earl of Ickenham, remains young at heart. So his jape of using a catapult to ping the silk top hat off his grumpy half-brother-in-law, is nothing out of the ordinary – but the consequences abound with possibilities.

UKRIDGE

Ukridge

Money makes the world go round for Stanley Featherstonehaugh Ukridge – looking like an animated blob of mustard in his bright yellow raincoat – and when there isn't enough of it, the world just has to spin a bit faster.

MR MULLINER

Meet Mr Mulliner

Sitting in the Angler's Rest, drinking hot scotch and lemon, Mr Mulliner has fabulous stories to tell of the extraordinary behaviour of his far-flung family. This includes Wilfred, whose formula for Buck-U-Uppo enables elephants to face tigers with the necessary nonchalance.

Mr Mulliner Speaking

Holding court in the bar-parlour of the Angler's Rest, Mr Mulliner reveals what happened to The Man Who Gave Up Smoking, what the Something Squishy was that the butler delivered on a silver salver, and what caused the dreadful Unpleasantness at Bludleigh Court.

MONTY BODKIN

The Luck of the Bodkins

Monty Bodkin, besotted with 'precious dream-rabbit' Gertrude Butterwick, Reggie and Ambrose Tennyson (the latter mistaken for the late Poet Laureate), and Hollywood starlet Lotus Blossom, complete with pet alligator, all embark on a voyage of personal discovery aboard the luxurious liner, *S. S. Atlantic*.

JEEVES
The Novels

Thank You, Jeeves

Bertie disappears to the country as a guest of his chum Chuffy – only to find his peace shattered by the arrival of his ex-fiancée Pauline Stoker, her formidable father and the eminent loony-doctor Sir Roderick Glossop. When Chuffy falls in love with Pauline and Bertie seems to be caught in flagrante, a situation boils up which only Jeeves (whether employed or not) can simmer down ...

Jeeves and the Feudal Spirit

A moustachioed Bertie must live up to 'Stilton' Cheesewright's expectations in the Drones Club darts tournament, or risk being beaten to a pulp by 'Stilton', jealous of his fiancée Florence's affections ...

Much Obliged, Jeeves

What happens when the Book of Revelations, the Junior Ganymede Club's recording of their masters' less than perfect habits, falls into potentially hostile hands?

Aunts Aren't Gentlemen

Under doctor's orders, Bertie moves with Jeeves to a countryside cottage. But Jeeves can cope with anything – even Aunt Dahlia.

Jeeves in the Offing

When Jeeves goes on holiday to Herne Bay, Bertie's life collapses; finding his mysterious engagement announced in *The Times* and encountering his nemesis Sir Roderick Glossop in disguise, Bertie hightails it to Herne Bay. Then the fun really starts ...

The Code of the Woosters

Purloining an antique cow creamer under the instruction of the indomitable Aunt Dahlia is the least of Bertie's tasks, for he has to play Cupid while feuding with Spode.

The Mating Season

In an idyllic Tudor manor in a picture-perfect English village, Bertie is in disguise as Gussie Fink-Nottle, Gussie is in disguise as Bertram Wooster and Jeeves, also in disguise, is the only one who can set things right ...

Ring for Jeeves

Patch Perkins and his clerk are not the 'honest bookies' they seem, but Bill, the rather impoverished Ninth Earl of Rowcester, and his temporary butler Jeeves. When they abscond with the freak winnings of Captain Biggar, Jeeves's resourcefulness is put to the test ...

Stiff Upper Lip, Jeeves

Bertie Wooster visits Major Plank in an attempt to return a work of art which Stiffy had told Bertie had been effectively stolen from Plank by Sir Watkyn Bassett. Thank goodness for Chief Inspector Witherspoon – but is he all he seems?

Right Ho, Jeeves

Bertie assumes his alter ego of Cupid and arranges the engagement of Gussie Fink-Nottle to Tuppy Glossop. Thankfully, Jeeves is ever present to correct the blundering plans hatched by his master.

Joy in the Morning

Trapped in rural Steeple Bumpleigh with old flame Florence Craye, her new and suspicious fiancé Stilton Cheesewright, and two-faced Edwin the Boy Scout, Bertie desperately needs Jeeves to save him ...

And Some Other Treats...

What Ho!

Introduced by Stephen Fry, this is a bumper anthology, providing the cream of the crop of Wodehouse's hilarious stories, together with verse, articles and all manner of treasures.

The Heart of a Goof

From his favourite chair on the terrace above the ninth hole, the Oldest Member reveals the stories behind his club's players, from notorious 'golfing giggler' Evangeline to poor, inept Rollo Podmarsh.

The Clicking of Cuthbert

A collection of stories, including that of Cuthbert, golfing ace, hopelessly in love with Adeline, who only cares for rising young writers. But enter a Great Russian Novelist with a strange passion, and Cuthbert's prospects might be looking up . . .

Big Money

Berry Conway, employee of dyspeptic American millionaire Torquil Patterson Frisby, has inherited a large number of shares in the Dream Come True copper mine. Of course they're worthless . . . aren't they?

Hot Water

In the heady atmosphere of a 1930s French chateau, J. Wellington Gedge only wants to return to his life in California, where everything is as it seems . . .

Laughing Gas

Joey Cooley, golden-curled Hollywood child film star, and six-foot-tall boxer Reginald, Earl of Havershot, are both under anaesthetic at the dentist's when their identities are swapped in the fourth dimension.

The Small Bachelor

It's Prohibition America and shy young George Finch is setting out as an artist – without the encumbrance of a shred of talent. Will George triumph over the social snob Mrs Waddington and successfully woo her stepdaughter?

Money for Nothing

Two households, both alike in dignity, in fair Rudge-in-the-Vale, where we lay our scene . . . Will the love of John Carmody and Pat Wyvern survive the bitter feud between their fathers, miserly Lester Carmody and peppery Colonel Wyvern?

Summer Moonshine

Poor Sir Buckstone Abbott owns in Walsingford Hall one of the least attractive stately homes in the country, so when a rich continental princess seems willing to buy it, he's overjoyed. But will the deal be completed?

The Adventures of Sally

When Sally Nicholas inherits some money, her life becomes increasingly complicated; with a needy brother, a handsome fiancé, who is not all he seems, and a naive generosity of spirit, Sally must turn to doting, clueless Ginger Kemp to set things right . . .

Young Men in Spats

Meet the Young Men in Spats – all innocent members of the Drones Club, all hopeless suitors, and all busy betting their sometimes non-existent fortunes on highly improbable outcomes. That is when they're not recovering from driving their sports cars *through* Marble Arch . . .

ALSO AVAILABLE IN THIS SERIES

Featuring

The Amazing Hat Mystery

Uncle Fred Flits By

Trouble Down at Tudsleigh

Featuring

Mulliner's Buck-U-Uppo

The Spot of Art

Strychnine in the Soup

Featuring

The Smile that Wins

Jeeves and the Song of Songs

The Great Sermon Handicap